Top Banana

by Cari Best

illustrated by Erika Oller

Orchard Books • New York

For David
from sumwun hoo cairz—*C.B.*

For Monica—*E.O.*

Text copyright © 1997 by Cari Best

Illustrations copyright © 1997 by Erika Oller

Orchard Books
95 Madison Avenue
New York, NY 10016

Manufactured in the United States of America
Printed by Barton Press, Inc.
Bound by Horowitz/Rae
Book design by Chris Hammill Paul

10   9   8   7   6   5   4   3   2   1

The text of this book is set in 17 point ITC Usherwood.
The illustrations are monotypes with pencil and
watercolor.

Library of Congress Cataloging-in-Publication Data

Best, Cari.
    Top banana / by Cari Best ; illustrated by Erika Oller.
        p.   cm.
    "A Melanie Kroupa book"—Half t.p.
    Summary: Benny the parrot, an amazing bird with
the ability to read, has everything a bird could want,
until he has to share his owner's attention with a rare
flower.
    ISBN 0-531-30009-9. — ISBN 0-531-33009-5 (lib. bdg.)
    [1. Parrots—Fiction. 2. Orchids—Fiction.
3. Jealousy—Fiction.]   I. Oller, Erika, ill.   II. Title.
PZ7.B46575To   1997
[E]—dc20   96-42286

EVERY DAY and twice on Sundays, Flora Dora's puny parrot, Benny, was the envy of every bird on the block.

Benny had a bright and airy room with a view, warm in winter and cool in summer.

He had nuts when he felt like nibbling,
fruits when he felt like chewing,
springwater for sipping, and some for bathing, too.

Flora dusted and polished and never forgot to spread a
clean sheet of newspaper on Benny's floor.

She took time away from her flowers to play games with him (hopscotch was Benny's favorite), turned on the kind of radio music that he liked to dance to,

and read him a story before he went to sleep. Two stories on Sundays. "Benito, my Benito," Flora cooed as she kissed him good-night. "You are the sweetest, most beautiful creature on earth. Your singing is divine. Your green is perfection. Your kisses are more delicate than my rarest roses. You are nature's masterpiece."

And every night before he closed his eyes,
Benny thanked his lucky stars for Flora.
Flora, who liked his chipper chirping.

Flora, who thought he looked
handsome even when he was wet or
molting.

Flora, who didn't get
angry if he nipped instead
of kissed. Flora, who loved him even
though he was just the chirping kind.

He couldn't say "I love you" back, but Benny returned Flora's favors in other ways. He fanned her when she felt faint. He helped fertilize her ferns. He fluted the edges of her fruit pies.

M E E O O O W W W w

And he entertained her with his clever impressions. At the drop of a hat, Benny could ring like a telephone, meow like a cat, scream like a fire engine, or serenade like a violin. Then Flora, his biggest fan, would cheer, "Bravo, Benito!" and shower him with rose petals. "You are the star of the show. You are my Top Banana." No bird could ask for more.

With all the attention Flora paid him, and all the stories she read him, Benny got to be so intelligent that, one day, he realized he could read.

Benny read weather reports and he read recipes. He read about improving his home and building his body, about bright ideas for the weekend and love boat cruises to Alaska. Benny read everything he could get his claws on.

Sometimes he would tear out interesting articles for Flora, whose nose was usually in her flowers. And sometimes he would tear out words:

HUGGER-MUGGER, PHOTOSYNTHESIS, CALISTHENICS.

When Flora found out he could read, she beamed. "Benito, Benito," she said. "You are indeed a rare bird."

One afternoon, when all the pansies were pinched and all the palms potted, Flora invited Benny out for a pedal. Benny jumped at the chance to check out the things he'd been reading about.

While Flora pointed out the fancy flowers, Benny noticed the fast cars, the flashing lights, the airplanes, and the street birds. My newspaper world has come alive! he chirped excitedly, wishing that he and Flora would go on pedaling forever. . . .

BOB'S BLOOMS

MY NAME IS SCARLETT O'HARA
I'M YOURS FOR THE ASKING

But something caught Flora's eye. "How much is that flower in the window?" she asked. "The one with the flaming red blooms, yellow spots, blue stripes, and frilly fringes?"

"She's a real tough cookie to grow," said Bob. "Likes her feet just so, the light just right, humidity on the high side, and fresh air blowing all around her. Exotic orchids like Scarlett O'Hara don't grow on trees, you know."

"We'll make her happy, won't we?" said Flora.

But Benny, who would rather have taken home the sunflower, wasn't so sure.

"Welcome to our little family," said Flora lovingly, strapping Scarlett in next to Benny in the Top Banana seat on the back of her bike, careful not to disturb a single pointy petal or puffy pouch.

So instead of seeing the world, as he had hoped, Benny and Flora . . . and Scarlett O'Hara headed for home.

Benny thought Scarlett was the fanciest flower he'd ever seen.

On Monday, he shared his view.

On Tuesday, his radio music.

On Wednesday, they all played hopscotch.

And on Thursday, they had a springwater shower.

On Friday, Benny did his duck impression.

And on Saturday, they baked a sour cherry pie.

On Sunday, when it was time for bed, Flora read to them both—two stories because it was Sunday. Then she kissed them both good-night. "You are the sweetest, most beautiful creatures on earth," she cooed. "Sleep tight, my nature's masterpieces."

I thought *I* was nature's masterpiece, Benny grumped. This sharing business is for the birds.

If only Scarlett would go back to Bob's, Benny wished. Then things would be just as they were.

He thought of putting her in the fridge,

hanging her in the closet,

or giving her a haircut.

Anything to be Flora's
Top Banana again.

Until one day, despite Flora's attention to Scarlett's feet, her light, the humidity and the air around her, no matter how many stories she read, Scarlett's blooms began to fade. Her frilly leaves fell. Her fringes drooped and her spots turned rusty. "It's not so easy growing an orchid," said Flora, looking quite frazzled.

Benny, who couldn't bear to see his Flora weep, wiped away her tears. What could be the matter? he wondered.

"We are losing our little Scarlett," Flora lamented.

Benny took a look at the once-beautiful exotic orchid. He couldn't believe his eyes. Was this sickly looking stalk of celery really Scarlett O'Hara? There must be some way to save her, he chirped.

So while Flora took Scarlett's temperature, Benny paced back and forth across the newspaper on his floor. ADD TO YOUR WARDROBE, SPRUCE UP YOUR MEALS, BOOST YOUR CAREER, he read. Words, words, words. None of them very helpful. What was wrong with Scarlett?

All of a sudden a headline caught his eye. "EARLY BIRD SPECIAL!" it said. "Fly away to the Hoochie Coochie Rain Forest, where there is always just the right amount of sun, rain, and tropical breeze. Ask any of our exotic orchids—they've been growing here for centuries!"

Exotic orchids? Growing there for centuries? That's it, Benny squawked. But when he showed the ad to Flora, her face fell. "Benito, bambino, our poor Scarlett is not well enough to make such a long trip."

Leave everything to me, Flora, my love, Benny chirped. And then he set to work.

EARLY BIRD SPECIAL

FLY AWAY TO THE HOOCHIE COOCHIE RAINFOREST

WHERE THERE IS ALWAYS JUST THE RIGHT AMOUNT OF SUN, AND A PERFECT TROPICAL BREEZE. ASK ANY OF OUR EXOTIC ORCHIDS— WE BEEN GROWING OR CENTURIES! . . .

ORCHID CARE COMPLETE

HAPPY ORCHIDS

Benny pushed and he pulled.

He lugged and he lifted.

He tore out and he turned on.

Before long, Flora understood what he was doing, and she joined in. "Benito, my Benito," she said. "You are a kind and thoughtful soul, and a bird with a very big brain." Flora's words were music to Benny's ears.

At long last they were all finished. There before them stood a perfectly glorious tropical rain forest—every bit as warm, wet, and windy as the Hoochie Coochie in the newspaper. For the first time in a very long time, Scarlett was all smiles. Benny and Flora were relieved to see her flaming red blooms, yellow spots, blue stripes, and frilly fringes slowly coming back.

"This calls for a celebration!" shouted Flora.

Then there was dancing (the Hoochie Coochie, of course) and
singing and swinging and laughing.

Benny did his howler monkey impression for Scarlett. (She loved it.) "Scarlett will be very happy here," said Flora, "and all because of you, my little lovebird."

Pretty soon Flora, who wasn't very fond of heat or humidity, excused herself to fix Benny a dinner to end all dinners—crispy lettuce, corn on the cob, and macaroni and cheese, all his favorites, while Benny, who found the hot, sticky climate very much to his liking, flew back and forth from the bathroom to the kitchen, splashing with Scarlett and flirting with Flora.

And that evening after their delicious dinner, Flora invited
Benny for a nice long pedal down a brand-new street,

and read him two stories before he went to sleep—even though it wasn't Sunday. And this time Benny didn't mind one bit that Scarlett listened, too.